WASHINGTON

HUSKIES

BY DAVE CAMPBELL

SportsZone

An Imprint of Abdo Publishing
abdopublishing.com

abdopublishing.com

Published by Abdo Publishing, a division of ABDO, PO Box 398166, Minneapolis, Minnesota 55439.

Printed in the United States of America, North Mankato, Minnesota
042018
092018

THIS BOOK CONTAINS RECYCLED MATERIALS

Cover Photo: Russell Lansford/Icon Sportswire/AP Images
Interior Photos: Thurman James/Cal Sports Media/AP Images, 4–5; Sean Brown/Cal Sports Media/AP Images, 6, 9; Mike Albright/Cal Sports Media/AP Images, 11; Michael Wade/Icon Sportswire/AP Images, 12; University of Southern California/Collegiate Images/Getty Images, 14–15; AP Images, 16, 21, 23, 27, 43 (top right), 43 (top middle), 43 (top left); Gene Herrick/AP Images, 18; Peter Read Miller/Sports Illustrated/Getty Images, 24–25; Bob Galbraith/AP Images, 28, 42 (bottom left); Otto Greule Jr/Getty Images, 32–33, 42 (bottom right); Tom Hauck/AP Images, 36–37; Ross D. Franklin/AP Images, 38, 43 (bottom right); Marcio Jose Sanchez/AP Images, 41; Barry Salmons/Shutterstock Images, 44

Editor: Julie Dick
Series Designer: Craig Hinton

Library of Congress Control Number: 2017962138

Publisher's Cataloging-in-Publication Data

Names: Campbell, Dave, author.
Title: Washington Huskies / by Dave Campbell.
Description: Minneapolis, Minnesota : Abdo Publishing, 2019. | Series: Inside college football | Includes online resources and index.
Identifiers: ISBN 9781532114649 (lib.bdg.) | ISBN 9781532154478 (ebook)
Subjects: LCSH: American football--Juvenile literature. | College sports--United States--History--Juvenile literature. | University of Washington. Huskies (Football team)--Juvenile literature. | Football--Records--United States--Juvenile literature.
Classification: DDC 796.332630--dc23

TABLE OF CONTENTS

Quarterback Jake Browning led the Huskies' offense in the 2016 season.

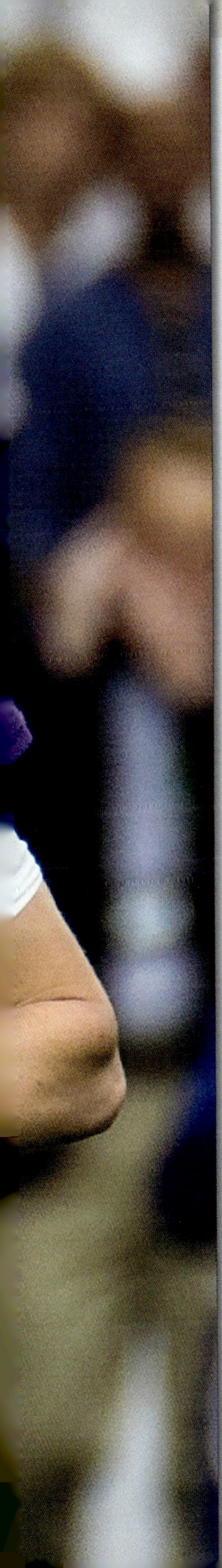

1

BACK ON THE BIG STAGE

THE FOOTBALL PROGRAM AT THE UNIVERSITY OF WASHINGTON WAS ON THE RISE AGAIN WHEN THE 2016 SEASON BEGAN. SOPHOMORE QUARTERBACK JAKE BROWNING WAS BACK AFTER GAINING VALUABLE EXPERIENCE AS A TRUE FRESHMAN STARTER. COACH CHRIS PETERSEN WAS BEGINNING HIS THIRD SEASON WITH THE HUSKIES AFTER BUILDING A STRONG RÉSUMÉ AT BOISE STATE.

Washington fans had high hopes. Popular opinion in the state and around the sport was that the Huskies were probably a year away from fully realizing their potential. Four games in, they were undefeated and ranked No. 10 in the country. Up to that point, though, none of their victories had been especially impressive.

Then came the matchup with seventh-ranked Stanford on September 30. The Cardinal had won their last three games against the Huskies. They had Heisman Trophy candidate

Wide receiver Aaron Fuller makes a touchdown catch against Stanford.

Christian McCaffrey in the backfield. And they had averaged 11 wins a year for the past six seasons.

But the Huskies had home-field advantage. The campus along the shores of Lake Washington was buzzing with excitement for a rare Friday night game. Fans throughout the city of Seattle and all over the Pacific Northwest settled in to watch.

That drama quickly disappeared. Browning threw three touchdown passes. Myles Gaskin rushed for two scores. The Huskies cruised to a 44–6 victory, showing their home crowd of 72,000 and a viewing audience on ESPN that they belonged back on the national stage. Washington produced its largest winning margin ever against a team ranked in the top 10.

How did the Huskies do it? For one thing, they limited McCaffrey to only 49 rushing yards, his lowest total in two years. For Stanford, the loss was its most lopsided in nine seasons. Huskies fans rushed onto the field in celebration after the final second ticked off the clock.

The signature victory didn't lead to a letdown, either. The following week, the Huskies went on the road to beat Oregon 70–21, ending

CHAMPION TITLES

The National Collegiate Athletic Association (NCAA) used to decide its Division I national championship on paper, not on the gridiron. Media organizations and coaching associations once conducted polls of their members to determine the national champion. In 1992 the NCAA began taking steps to ensure that the No. 1 and No. 2 teams would face off in a bowl game to determine the national title on the field.

After trying other methods, the College Football Playoff (CFP) began in 2014. It was the first system to include more than two teams. The 13-member CFP committee ranks the top 25 teams in each of the last six weeks of the season. The final four is revealed after the conference championship games are played. Semifinals are played on the site of two of the six "major" bowl games. The winners meet a week later to determine the national champion.

BROWNING'S BACKGROUND

Chris Petersen and his offensive coordinator, Jonathan Smith, began recruiting Jake Browning while they were still coaching at Boise State. When Petersen and Smith arrived at Washington before the 2014 season, the 6-foot-2, 210-pound quarterback from Folsom, California, was a top priority. Browning set several national records in high school, including 91 touchdown passes in his final year. In 2015 he became the Huskies' first true freshman to win the starting quarterback job. The next year, Browning earned the Pac-12 Offensive Player of the Year Award. He also took sixth place in the Heisman Trophy voting. That was the second-highest finish of any Washington player.

a 12-game losing streak to the rival Ducks. Browning was in a groove by now. He passed for 304 yards and a school-record six touchdowns that night. Three went to John Ross. Two were to Dante Pettis.

The Huskies finished October ranked No. 4 in the nation after a win at No. 17 Utah. Browning matched his program record in the next game, with another six touchdown passes to beat California. But a matchup with the University of Southern California (USC) was not to be overlooked. No team has dominated the Pac-12 Conference like the Trojans have. USC's 2016 squad wasn't its best, but they still proved to be a difficult test.

The Huskies were already missing defensive end Joe Mathis, their top pass-rusher, who had hurt his foot in practice after the Oregon game. He eventually needed surgery. Then standout linebacker Azeem Victor broke a bone in his lower leg while trying to make a tackle. He had to ride on a cart to leave the field and had surgery eventually, too. Those absences took some strength out

The Huskies defense put the clamps on rival Washington State in 2016.

of the Washington defense. Trojans quarterback Sam Darnold and his offensive line handled the pass rush well. USC went on to win 26–13.

The loss knocked the Huskies back to No. 7 in the Associated Press (AP) poll. More important, they dropped to sixth in the playoff rankings. The top four teams at the end of the season get to compete for the national title. So the Huskies went back to work, realizing another defeat would ruin their chance of a top-four ranking.

First, Washington responded with a smooth win over Arizona State and climbed to fifth. Then the Huskies traveled across the Cascade Mountains to Washington State for the Apple Cup game. This was the 109th meeting between the two rivals. The Huskies had won 70 of the previous matchups, a decisive edge in the in-state series. The Cougars, however, had put together a solid season behind quarterback Luke Falk and coach Mike Leach. The Cougars entered the game ranked No. 23 in the country. That made this only the sixth time in history that both Washington and Washington State played as top-25 teams. The winner would take the Pac-12 North Division title.

The Huskies were up to the task. They intercepted three of Falk's passes. They stopped the Cougars inside the 10-yard line three times. They piled up more than 500 total yards. They left the town of Pullman with a 45–17 victory and a spot in the Pac-12 championship game. There was more good news, too. With two teams ahead of them in the CFP rankings, Ohio State and Michigan, playing each other that weekend, one had to lose. Michigan fell, and the Huskies climbed past the Wolverines into fourth place.

APPLE CUP

The state of Washington is known for producing apples. So it makes sense that the state's two largest schools would play for a trophy called the Apple Cup. Every year in late November, Washington and Washington State renew their rivalry. The teams met for the first time in 1900. They have played every year since 1945. The Huskies' victory in 2017 gave them a 72–32–6 record in the series.

Huskies fans at the Pac-12 championship looked forward to a potential showdown with Alabama.

That left one more game between them and a coveted spot in the CFP. Ninth-ranked Colorado won the Pac-12 South Division, so the Buffaloes and Huskies squared off in Santa Clara, California, at the San Francisco 49ers' stadium. The Huskies probably needed just a win to hold onto the last CFP spot. But a decisive victory would show the CFP selection committee the Huskies were worthy of a top-four spot.

The Huskies charge out of the tunnel to face Alabama in the Peach Bowl.

And that's exactly what they delivered. Gaskin had 159 rushing yards and Lavon Coleman added 101 more. Taylor Rapp had two interceptions on defense. One of them he took back for a touchdown. The Huskies were conference champions for the first time in 16 years after their 41–10 victory.

Two days later, it was official: Washington was picked as the fourth team in the playoffs. The Huskies were pitted against top-ranked Alabama in the Peach Bowl. Clemson and Ohio State were matched up in the other semifinal.

In some ways, making it this far was a bonus for the Huskies. They were two-touchdown underdogs against the Crimson Tide. Alabama had won three bowl series championships under coach Nick Saban. But the Huskies didn't go to Atlanta for a vacation. Win or lose, this was going to be another defining game in the redevelopment of the program under Petersen.

The Crimson Tide used their stingy defense and bruising running attack to wear down the Huskies that night. Browning threw a touchdown pass to Pettis on the opening drive for Washington. But that's all the offense the Huskies could generate. Alabama forced three turnovers and held the Huskies to just 194 total yards in a 24–7 victory.

The Huskies finished the season with a 12–2 record. It didn't end the way they wanted it to, but expectations for the future under Petersen's leadership were raised even higher.

PETTIS'S PUNT RETURNS

The Huskies took a big hit on their quest to return to the CFP in the 2017 season when they lost at Arizona State on October 14. A loss to Stanford on November 10 ended their chance at a national championship. There were still plenty of highlights, though, starting with Dante Pettis. In a big win over Oregon, he set the NCAA record with his ninth career punt return for a touchdown.

The Huskies and USC square off at the Los Angeles Memorial Coliseum in 1926.

2

ONE-EYED BOB

THE FIRST RECORDED FOOTBALL GAME IN WASHINGTON HISTORY WAS IN 1889. BUT GIL DOBIE PUT THE PROGRAM ON THE MAP 20 YEARS LATER. DOBIE WAS WASHINGTON'S HEAD COACH FROM 1908 TO 1916. HIS TEAMS NEVER LOST A GAME, WINNING 58 AND TYING THREE. IN FACT, WASHINGTON HOLDS THE ALL-TIME NCAA DIVISION I RECORD FOR THE LONGEST UNBEATEN STREAK AT 64 GAMES. THE HUSKIES WON 60 AND TIED FOUR BETWEEN 1907 AND 1917, WITH DOBIE ON THE SIDELINES FOR MOST OF THAT SPAN.

However, he often had trouble fitting in. Dobie was known as a strict man with an unfriendly demeanor. He stalked the sideline during games with a cigar and a trench coat. Despite his success on the field, his attitude made him unpopular with the fans. When he had meetings with his quarterbacks, he didn't allow them to speak.

Dobie was as old-fashioned as they came. Years later, when he was the head coach at Cornell, his team lost a game

Three Huskies defenders close in on Pittsburgh running back Marshall Goldberg in the 1937 Rose Bowl.

to Dartmouth 62–13. But in his mind, Cornell had won 13–0. "I don't count those scores made by passing," he said, displaying his trademark refusal to adapt to change. "That isn't football."

Dobie left Washington for the head coaching job at Navy before moving on to Cornell and Boston College. The Huskies soon recovered from his departure, and after a couple of down seasons, new coach Enoch Bagshaw turned them into champions. From 1922 to 1925, Bagshaw's Huskies won 34 games, lost just four, and tied four. They also played in two Rose Bowls with George "Wildcat" Wilson as their star running back.

After going 10–1 in 1923, Washington met Navy at the Rose Bowl on New Year's Day. Trailing 14–7 in the fourth quarter, the Huskies recovered a fumble at the Navy 12-yard line. Three running plays went nowhere, but on fourth down halfback Fred Abel passed to James Bryan for a touchdown, and the game ended in a 14–14 tie.

"BOW DOWN"

In 1915 a former Washington student named Lester Wilson wrote "Bow Down to Washington" for the student newspaper's school fight song contest. The lyrics have changed over the years, but the title is the same. Here's the first verse of the modern version:

Bow down to Washington
Bow down to Washington
Mighty are the men who wear the
purple and the gold
Joyfully we welcome them within the
victor's fold
We will carve their names in the Hall
of Fame
To preserve the memory of
our devotion

Two years later, Washington was back in the Rose Bowl after winning the Pacific Coast Conference (PCC) with a 10–0–1 record. On January 1, 1926, in what is widely considered one of the best Rose Bowls ever played, the heavily favored Huskies lost to Alabama 20–19. Wilson was knocked unconscious in the second quarter and was carried off the field on a stretcher. The Crimson Tide scored all of their points in the third quarter when Wilson was missing. He returned in the fourth quarter to lead a Huskies rally that came up just short.

Those glory days of the 1920s gave way to a rather mediocre three decades of football in Seattle. The one exception was in 1936, when

Hugh McElhenny plunges through the line to score a touchdown against Montana in 1951.

coach James Phelan led the Huskies back to the Rose Bowl by winning the PCC with a 7–1–1 mark. After a season-opening loss to Minnesota, the only blemish on Washington's schedule the rest of the way was a tie with Stanford. Washington closed the season with shutout victories over USC and Washington State, both ranked in the top 20 at the time.

But the Huskies were throttled by third-ranked Pittsburgh 21–0 in the Rose Bowl and settled for being ranked No. 5 in the nation in the season's final poll.

In the early 1950s, running back Hugh McElhenny put together one of the best two-year stretches in Washington program history. Many of McElhenny's records still stood through 2017, including his 296 rushing yards in a 1950 game against Washington State. And his 100-yard punt return for a touchdown in 1951 against USC will never be topped.

"He opened up the game, lifted the action to a higher level," his quarterback Don Heinrich once said. "He made our offense a lot more fun."

Finally, on January 1, 1960, Washington scored its first Rose Bowl victory. The first of two straight 10–1 seasons under head coach Jim Owens sent the eighth-ranked Huskies back to Pasadena to face No. 6 Wisconsin.

Rugged quarterback Bob Schloredt was Washington's star player. Schloredt was legally blind in his left eye. The disability dated back to his childhood. He and one of his friends were fooling around with firecrackers. They put one in a jar and it exploded, sending a shard of glass into Schloredt's left eye. He lost all but about five percent of his vision in that eye, but he didn't miss out on much.

"My folks never made anything of it, and I always did everything the other kids were doing," Schloredt said in a *Sports Illustrated* cover story about him that was published during his senior season in 1960.

His ability on the field made it easy to forget that he was blind in one eye. "To tell you the truth, I didn't even know he had one eye at the time we recruited him," said Owens, who arrived at the university at the same time as Schloredt in 1957.

Schloredt was more of a runner than a thrower. Back then, passing schemes were far less complex than they are now. His strength was his toughness. That allowed him to star as a defensive player as well. As a junior in 1959, he made significant strides as a passer and as a leader.

The Huskies were smaller and less experienced than Wisconsin. But they used their quickness to beat the Badgers 44–8. Schloredt was named a first team All-American that year. His senior season was limited by injury, but he returned in time for another Rose Bowl.

WHAT'S IN A NAME?

The Pac-12 Conference changed its name from the Pac-10 in 2011 when Colorado and Utah entered the league. The conference was previously called the Pac-8, until Arizona and Arizona State joined in 1978. The other eight teams—Washington, Washington State, Oregon, Oregon State, California, Stanford, USC, and the University of California, Los Angeles (UCLA) have been together in a league continuously since 1964. They were first grouped in 1928, when Idaho and Montana also competed in what was then the Pacific Coast Conference. Idaho and Montana eventually moved to a lower level. From 1959 to 1967, the core members of the conference competed as the Athletic Association of Western Universities. In 1968 the conference changed its name to the Pac-8.

Quarterback Bob Schloredt was a two-time Rose Bowl Most Valuable Player (MVP).

This time, the opponent was mighty Minnesota. The Gophers were already considered national champions, because the final national poll vote took place before the bowl games. Led by quarterback Sandy Stephens, the Gophers were an even more physically imposing opponent than Wisconsin was.

Owens was ready with a savvy game plan. Schloredt and his teammates were plenty confident. The Huskies took a 17–0 lead and played safe enough in the second half to stay in front. Even though the Gophers outgained them 192–35 in second-half yardage, they managed only one touchdown. The Huskies held on for a 17–7 victory.

SONNY SIXKILLER

Washington's history is rich with standout quarterbacks. Among the big names, few are more memorable than Sonny Sixkiller. When he became a starter as a sophomore in 1970 (wearing jersey No. 6, of course), he helped lead a shift in philosophy under head coach Jim Owens. The Huskies had finished 1–9 in 1969 while running a wishbone offense. With Sixkiller behind center, they began to mix in more passes. In his first start against Michigan State, on the first play, Sixkiller completed a 15-yard pass. The crowd at Husky Stadium roared.

"Coach Owens had a reputation for being a 'three-yards-and-a-cloud-of-dust' kind of guy," Sixkiller said of his coach's conservative leanings. "But here we were throwing the ball one play into the season."

Washington's record over three seasons with Sixkiller as the quarterback was 22–10. Through 2017 he still ranked second in Huskies history with a career average of 196.3 passing yards per game.

Sonny Sixkiller brought his flashy game to Washington in 1970.

As sportswriter Red Smith declared in his account in the *New York Herald Tribune*, "The swift Washington backs raced over, past, and around the meaty monsters of the Midwest, who seemed to be moving in hip boots." Schloredt was named the MVP of the Rose Bowl for a second straight time. He was the first player ever to win multiple Rose Bowl MVP Awards.

Future Hall of Fame quarterback Warren Moon first made a name for himself with the Huskies.

3

CHAMPIONS

OF ALL THE PEOPLE IN HISTORY WHO HELPED ESTABLISH WASHINGTON AS A PREMIER FOOTBALL PROGRAM, DON JAMES LEADS THE LIST. HE'S KNOWN BY HUSKIES FANS AS SIMPLY "THE DAWGFATHER."

The head coach at Washington from 1975 to 1992, James enjoyed his first taste of success during the 1977 season. The Huskies started 1–3 in nonconference play. Then a 54–0 win at Oregon on October 8 got them going. They lost only once more, against UCLA. Washington punched its Rose Bowl ticket with a 35–15 win over Washington State. Then the Huskies beat Michigan 27–20 in Pasadena. James was named the national coach of the year by the American Football Coaches Association.

His quarterback, Warren Moon, was a key player in that triumph. Moon was the first prized recruit that James secured at Washington. He persuaded Moon to come north

WRONG NAME

Don James was hired only after several other candidates turned down the job in 1975. He'd been an assistant at Florida State, Michigan, and Colorado. His head coaching experience, however, was limited to four seasons at Kent State in Ohio. When James and his wife, Carol, arrived on campus for his formal interview, the Husky Stadium marquee displayed this message: "Welcome Don Jones."

after a year at West Los Angeles Junior College. Moon was black, and at the time most people in the football world thought that black players couldn't handle the demands of playing quarterback. James didn't believe that. He supported Moon as the quarterback adjusted to a higher level of competition, even as Huskies fans grew restless about Moon's performance. James's trust paid off. Moon was picked as the conference Player of the Year and the Rose Bowl MVP for that special 1977 season.

James led the Huskies back to the Rose Bowl in 1980 and 1981. In 1984 they were ranked No. 1 in the country for four weeks before a loss to USC knocked them out of the running for the national title. They had to "settle" for finishing with the No. 2 ranking after beating Oklahoma 28–17 in the Orange Bowl.

But James's last teams were among the best ever to play at Washington. From 1990 to 1992, the Huskies won three straight Pac-10 Conference titles and played in the Rose Bowl each year. But 1991 was special even by those standards. Ask anyone in Washington which team won college football's national championship that year, and the Huskies would be the easy answer. Most followers of the sport around

Warren Moon and Don James celebrate after the 1978 Rose Bowl victory.

the country even felt that way. A handful of organizations, including the prominent Coaches Poll, voted Washington No. 1 that season.

However, the AP poll of national media members produced a different winner: Miami. Both teams had a 12–0 record, so each side made a strong argument for being ranked No. 1. Even James would've had a hard time denying the Hurricanes their due. That's because he played his college football at Miami in the early 1950s.

Mark Bruener (85) celebrates a touchdown catch during the 1992 Rose Bowl.

The lower divisions of college football use a national tournament to determine a winner on the field. The NCAA's top level had only one way to crown a champion: with a vote. Washington was matched up against Michigan in the Rose Bowl on New Year's Day 1992. Miami went to the Orange Bowl to face Nebraska. Unless the Hurricanes were upset on their home field, the only way the Huskies could be the consensus national champion was with a convincing victory.

That's exactly what they delivered in Pasadena that day. They beat the Wolverines 34–14. They sacked Michigan quarterback Elvis Grbac six times in that game. Going into the game, he'd been sacked only six times *all season*. After the game, Grbac said the Huskies were the "best team I've ever played by far."

But the AP voters still favored Miami. The Hurricanes flattened Nebraska 22–0 and were considered to have played a more difficult schedule. They had beaten the No. 1 team at the time, Florida State, in mid-November.

These Huskies, however, were a once-in-a-generation group. Napoleon Kaufman was a budding star as a freshman running back. Billy Joe Hobert had taken over for the injured Mark Brunell and thrived at quarterback. Mario Bailey was an All-American wide receiver. Lincoln Kennedy was the giant offensive tackle anchoring the line.

STATUE UNVEILED

The university made permanent Don James's place in Huskies history on October 27, 2017, when it unveiled an 8-foot-6-inch (2.6-m.) statue of James standing with his arms crossed. He's wearing a determined look and his signature cap with the Washington "W" on the front. Warren Moon was on hand for the ceremony, among hundreds of other former players.

"He wasn't just a football coach that developed players. He was a football coach who developed young men," Moon said during his speech that day.

Then there was that punishing defense. Steve Emtman was its star. He was a 290-pound defensive tackle with an elite blend of speed and strength. He was almost impossible to block one-on-one. He finished with 20½ tackles for loss that season. Emtman won the Lombardi Award, given to the best defensive lineman or linebacker in the country.

He also took home the Outland Trophy, given to the nation's top interior lineman. Behind Emtman's strong play up front, Huskies defense allowed an average of only 9.2 points per game that season.

Less than two years after the Huskies reached the peak of their sport, they slipped a bit. In the summer of 1993, the Pac-10 Conference placed the program on probation. The Huskies were punished for NCAA rule violations made by multiple players. Some were said to have used more university money for meals and entertainment than they were allowed. Some worked jobs for Huskies fans, who paid them more than they were supposed to. Hobert was found to have accepted a $50,000 loan from a businessman.

HEY, BROTHER

Many top-flight quarterbacks have played for the Huskies. Two of them even had the same last name. Damon Huard first came to the program in 1992 under Don James. His brother Brock Huard arrived in 1996, when Jim Lambright was the head coach. Both Huard brothers went on to play in the NFL. Brock is fourth all-time in Huskies history in passing yards. Damon is sixth.

The punishment included a two-year ban on playing in bowl games. James was upset. He wanted to be able to speak with the accused players before the conference announced the penalties. The university also felt the punishment by the Pac-10 was too harsh. James decided to retire at the end of the season.

The replacement for the legendary James had a tall task in front of him. Fortunately, he was already on the staff. Jim Lambright was the defensive coordinator for the Huskies at the time. He'd been an assistant with the program for 25 years. He had also played for the Huskies in the early 1960s. He was a lifelong resident of the state of Washington. Initially, Lambright was promoted to head coach on an interim basis. Eventually, the university made the hire official.

Lambright lasted six seasons as head coach. The Huskies played in a bowl game in each of the four years they were eligible, but their best record under Lambright's leadership was 9–3 in 1996. The standard had been set higher under James. There was pressure on the university to pick a new coach. Still, Lambright left behind a lot of admirers. "This was the most difficult decision I ever made here at the University of Washington," his boss, athletic director Barbara Hedges, said after firing Lambright.

The highlight of Lambright's tenure came in 1994, when he guided the Huskies to one of their most memorable regular-season wins in history. It also gave them a bit of revenge for their 1991 snub. Miami had an NCAA-record 58-game winning streak at the Orange Bowl, their home stadium. But the Huskies snapped that streak with a resounding 38–20 victory.

Rick Neuheisel was the Huskies' head coach from 1999 to 2002.

4

FURTHER CONCERNS

JIM LAMBRIGHT'S REPLACEMENT WAS A FORMER UCLA QUARTERBACK NAMED RICK NEUHEISEL. HE KNEW THE PAC-10 LANDSCAPE WELL AND AT AGE 37 WAS ONE OF THE FIVE HIGHEST-PAID HEAD COACHES IN THE COUNTRY. HIS SEVEN-YEAR CONTRACT CALLED FOR A $1 MILLION SALARY. NEUHEISEL HAD POSTED A 33–14 RECORD AT COLORADO BEFORE DECIDING TO MOVE WEST TO WASHINGTON.

One of the first decisions Neuheisel made drew instant praise from his players. He switched the color of the team's helmets from purple back to the gold headgear they had used under James. In 2000, Neuheisel's second season with the Huskies, they finished 11–1 after a Rose Bowl victory over Purdue. They were ranked No. 3 in the final AP poll.

Quarterback Marques Tuiasosopo was the MVP in his final college game. He used his trademark mix of running and passing to wear down Purdue's defense. He even played through a shoulder injury that sidelined him for a few plays.

Tuiasosopo finished with 1,495 rushing yards for his career. That was a record for a Huskies quarterback at the time. His replacement, Cody Pickett, joined him in the record books by setting many of the program's passing records. As a junior in 2002, Pickett passed for 4,458 yards, an average of 343 per game. He considered leaving school early for the NFL draft, but Neuheisel persuaded him to stay for his senior year. Pickett wound up tearing a pectoral muscle in the second game. He played through the injury, but it affected his performance.

The 2000 season was the high point on the field for the Huskies under Neuheisel, however. They went 8–4 and 7–6 the following two years. They were defeated in minor bowl games each time.

TUIASOSOPO TAKES OFF

Marques Tuiasosopo was recruited in high school by several schools interested in making him a safety or even a linebacker. Colorado was one of those when Neuheisel was there. But the Huskies were committed to keeping him at quarterback.

Tuiasosopo played his breakout game as a junior on October 30, 1999. He carried Washington to an upset of Stanford. Despite a hip injury he suffered in the first quarter that sent him to the locker room for treatment, Tuiasosopo rushed for 207 yards. He also passed for 302 yards. That made him the first player in major college football history with a 300/200 game. The 509 total yards easily beat Cary Conklin's single-game record, set 10 years prior with 419 total yards. He did all that with a limp from the injury.

"It was the most amazing thing I've ever seen a football player do," wide receiver Dane Looker said that day. "What he pulled off today was miraculous."

Neuheisel's energetic and confident style rubbed some people the wrong way. His critics nicknamed him "Slick Rick." He did wrong at times, too. Both Colorado and Washington were placed on NCAA probation for rules violations that took place under his leadership.

Then came his ultimate undoing in 2003. Neuheisel was found to have bet money on high-stakes NCAA basketball pools he was not allowed to participate in. He said he didn't realize he was breaking a rule. He initially lied about his involvement, however. That's what led to his firing.

The story didn't stop there. Neuheisel eventually sued the university for wrongful termination. He won a $4.5 million settlement in court. The case took 21 months to play out.

"I feel fully vindicated," Neuheisel said outside the courtroom after the verdict was reached by the jury. "Obviously they're going to have their stories, too, but I feel like this is the best scenario."

Strong-armed quarterback Jake Locker was also a running threat during his days with the Huskies.

5

REBUILDING

RICK NEUHEISEL'S FIRING LED TO ANOTHER ROUGH PERIOD FOR THE HUSKIES. HIS REPLACEMENT, KEITH GILBERTSON, WAS LET GO AFTER FINISHING 1–10 IN HIS SECOND SEASON. TYRONE WILLINGHAM, WHO'D BEEN AT STANFORD AND NOTRE DAME PREVIOUSLY, WAS HIRED IN 2005. HIS TEAMS WENT A COMBINED 11–37, INCLUDING AN 0–12 RECORD IN 2008.

That led to the hiring of another up-and-comer in the coaching ranks: 34-year-old Steve Sarkisian. Sarkisian came from conference rival USC, where he was quarterback coach for Heisman Trophy award winners Carson Palmer and Matt Leinart.

Like Neuheisel before him, Sarkisian's arrival reenergized the program and the fans. "Bark for Sark" shirts were seen on campus and around Seattle. In his first season, Sarkisian guided quarterback Jake Locker to a breakout junior year for Washington. It led to him being selected in the first round of the NFL draft.

Chris Petersen coaches players before the 2017 Fiesta Bowl.

After an 8–4 finish in the regular season in 2013, however, Sarkisian headed south. He stunned the Huskies players and fans by taking the job as head coach at USC, returning to his roots. So Huskies quarterback coach Marques Tuiasosopo led the team in the Fight Hunger Bowl against Brigham Young. He helped the Huskies win their first postseason game since the Rose Bowl win over Purdue 13 years earlier.

The seeds had been sown for a return to Pac-12 prominence, but Sarkisian's departure disappointed fans. Washington turned east for his replacement, hiring Chris Petersen away from Boise State in 2013.

Petersen had helped bring Boise State into the mix with some of the nation's best teams, despite the Broncos playing in a lower-tier conference. Boise State had two undefeated seasons under Petersen, winning the Fiesta Bowl after the 2006 and 2009 seasons. Many bigger programs came after him. He resisted their calls until Washington made him an offer he could not refuse.

2017 UPDATE

The Huskies won their first six games of the 2017 season and were ranked as high as No. 5 in the national polls. They finished the regular season 10–2 but lost a 35–28 shootout to Penn State in the Fiesta Bowl.

"It was just time. We had done some really good things there. And for me to take that next step as a coach, as a teacher, as a person, to grow I needed to take that next step out of that comfort zone over there," Petersen said as he was introduced.

The beginning of Petersen's second season with the Huskies was tough. He had to take his new team on the road to face his old one in Boise. There, the Broncos proved to be ungracious hosts. The Huskies trailed 16–0 at halftime, before a second-half rally fell short in a 16–13 defeat.

The Huskies were just 7–6 that season, with five losses in Pac-12 play. But they won their final three games, including a 45–10 victory over rival Washington State for the Apple Cup. Progress was taking place. The Huskies were about to break out in 2016, and the future never looked brighter in Seattle.

LOUD BY THE LAKE

Husky Stadium is considered one of the greatest settings in college football. It overlooks Lake Washington just 5 miles (8 km) north of downtown Seattle. It has gorgeous mountain views to the east and west. Seventy percent of the seats are located between the end zones. They're covered by a partial metal roof that traps the crowd noise and turns the venue into one of the loudest in the game. With an official seating capacity of 70,138, Husky Stadium ranks in the top 15 largest on-campus facilities. It was most recently remodeled in 2013 for $280 million. It was built in 1920 for $600,000. Adjusted for inflation to 2013 dollars, that was still only about $7 million.

"When recruits come in here, I don't know where else they're going to go in the country and see better," Steve Sarkisian said after the renovation was completed.

One of the most unique aspects of Husky Stadium is the waterside access. The university allows up to 150 private boats to dock near the shore or drop anchor and tailgate in the bay. There's a shuttle service available to take fans from their boats to the dock.

Dante Pettis shrugs off a Stanford tackler in a 2017 game.

TIMELINE

1900

The Huskies face rival Washington State for the first time, recording a 5–5 tie on November 30.

1907

The Huskies finish the season in a scoreless tie with Idaho on November 28. This starts a 64-game unbeaten streak.

1917

The unbeaten streak ends with a 27–0 loss at California on November 3.

1920

The first game in Husky Stadium is played on November 27, a 28–7 loss to Dartmouth.

1924

Washington ties with Navy in its first Rose Bowl on January 1.

1982

Washington beats Iowa 28–0 in the Rose Bowl on January 1 to finish another 10–2 season and is ranked No. 10 in the final AP poll.

1985

The Huskies rally for a 28–17 victory over favored Oklahoma in the Orange Bowl on January 1 to land a No. 2 final ranking for the season.

1992

Washington defeats Michigan in the Rose Bowl on January 1 to finish the season 12–0 and ranked No. 1 in the Coaches Poll.

1993

The Huskies lose the Rose Bowl game to Michigan on January 1.

1999

Head coach Rick Neuheisel wins his first game against his former team Colorado on September 25.

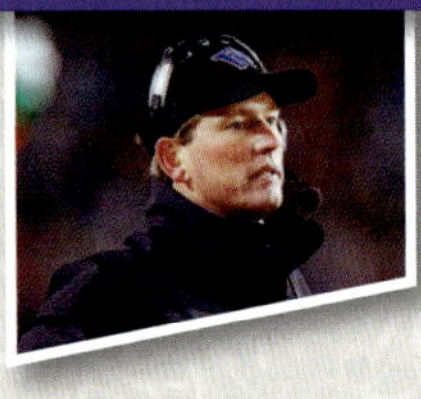

The Huskies play in the Rose Bowl against Pittsburgh January 1.

1937

Washington and Washington State play on October 13 and November 24, beginning the Apple Cup competition.

1945

The Huskies secure their first Rose Bowl victory against Wisconsin 44–8 on January 1.

1960

The Huskies win their first Apple Cup game under head coach Don James with a last-minute touchdown pass.

1975

The Huskies defeat the Michigan Wolverines 27–20 in the Rose Bowl January 1.

1978

Washington's only loss of the season comes on September 30 at Oregon.

2000

Washington loses to Baylor 67–56 in the Alamo Bowl on December 29.

2011

Washington opens the season with a win over San Diego State on September 1.

2012

New head coach Chris Petersen makes his debut with a 17–16 victory at Hawaii on August 30.

2014

The Huskies play in the Pac-12 championship game for the first time, beating Colorado 41–10 on December 2.

2016

QUICK STATS

PROGRAM INFO*

University of Washington
Various nicknames, 1889–1918
Sun Dodgers, 1919–21
Huskies, 1922–present

NATIONAL CHAMPIONSHIPS

1991 (USA Today/CNN Coaches Poll)

OTHER ACHIEVEMENTS

NCAA Division I record longest unbeaten streak: 64 straight games (1907–17)
Conference championships: 16 (five ties)
Rose Bowl appearances: 14 (7–6–1 record)
All-time bowl record: 17–18–1

KEY PLAYERS
(POSITION, SEASONS WITH TEAM)

Steve Emtman (DT, 1989–91)
Brock Huard (QB, 1996–98)
Lincoln Kennedy (OT, 1989–92)
Hugh McElhenny (RB, 1949–51)
Warren Moon (QB, 1975–77)
Chuck Nelson (PK, 1980–82)
Cody Pickett (QB, 1999–2003)
Bob Schloredt (QB, 1958–60)
Marques Tuiasosopo (QB, 1997–2000)
George Wilson (RB, 1923–25)

KEY COACHES

Enoch Bagshaw (1921–29)
64–21–6 (bowl record: 0–1–1)
Gil Dobie (1908–16)
59–0–3
Don James (1975–92)
150–60–2 (bowl record: 10–4)
Jim Owens (1957–74)
99–82–6 (bowl record: 2–1)
James Phelan (1930–41)
65–37–8 (bowl record: 0–1)

HOME STADIUM

Denny Field (1895–1920)
Husky Stadium (1920–)

*statistics through 2017 season

QUOTES & ANECDOTES

Husky Hall of Fame member Herman Brix was known for more than just football. He was a standout offensive tackle for the team and played in the 1926 Rose Bowl. But he also starred for the track and field team. He even won a silver medal in the shot put at the 1928 Olympics. Then came his bigger claim to fame. Brix, who took the stage name Bruce Bennett, later became an actor. He appeared in more than 100 movies. One of his career highlights was earning the starring role in *The New Adventures of Tarzan* in 1935.

The Seattle Seahawks played their home games at Husky Stadium in 2000 and 2001 while their new stadium was being built. The Seahawks paid the university $305,000 per game. The Seahawks returned the favor in 2012, hosting the Huskies' home games while the university remodeled.

"He was a special man and meant the world to me. There aren't enough words to describe not only the great coach he was, but how much he cared for people and the positive impact he made in the lives of everyone he came in contact with. Coach James was my mentor and probably did more to influence me in this profession."—Alabama head coach Nick Saban, after the death of Don James in 2013. Saban played for James at Kent State in the early 1970s.

GLOSSARY

All-American
Designation for players chosen as the best amateurs in the country in a particular sport.

backfield
The area where the quarterback and running backs begin each play.

bowl game
A game after the season that teams earn the right to play in by having a good season.

draft
A system that allows teams to acquire new players coming into a league.

end zone
The 10-yard portion of the field at each end a player must reach to score a touchdown.

lineman
A player on either offense or defense who starts each play closest to the ball, usually crouched in a stance with one hand on the ground.

ranking
A national position as determined by voters.

rival
An opponent with whom a player or team has a fierce and ongoing competition.

sack
To tackle the quarterback behind the line of scrimmage before he can pass the ball.

true freshman
An athlete who plays during his or her first year of college.

underdog
The person or team that is not expected to win.

wishbone
An offensive style that features a quarterback, a fullback, and two halfbacks, all of whom are threats to run the ball.

FOR MORE INFORMATION

ONLINE RESOURCES

Booklinks
NONFICTION NETWORK
FREE! ONLINE NONFICTION RESOURCES

To learn more about the Washington Huskies, visit abdobooklinks.com. These links are routinely monitored and updated to provide the most current information available.

BOOKS

Jude, Adam. *100 Things Washington Fans Should Know & Do before They Die.* Chicago, IL: Triumph Books, 2017.

Porter, W. Thomas. *Go Huskies! Celebrating Washington's Football Tradition.* Chicago, IL: Triumph Books, 2013.

Wilner, Barry. *Total Football.* Minneapolis, MN: Abdo Publishing, 2017.

PLACE TO VISIT

Alaska Airlines Field at Husky Stadium
3800 Montlake Blvd. NE
Seattle, WA 98195
206-543-2200
gohuskies.com

This has been Washington's home stadium since 1920, having undergone renovations in 1950, 1987, and 2012. Sponsor Alaska Airlines bought naming rights in 2015 for $41 million over 10 years. Tours are available with advance registration on Tuesdays and Thursdays, depending on stadium availability.

INDEX

ABOUT THE AUTHOR

Dave Campbell has been a Minnesota-based sportswriter for the Associated Press since 2000, after he graduated from the University of St. Thomas in St. Paul, Minnesota. He has followed college football since kindergarten, when he began to memorize team nicknames and track conference standings on fall Saturdays.